Cuddle Bear

Claire Freedman

Gavin Scott

LITTLE TIGER PRESS
London

If you feel a little sad,
Or lonely, lost and blue,
Don't worry, call for Cuddle Bear...

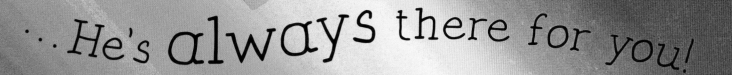

...He's **always** there for you!

Do you need cuddles, cheer-up hugs,
Or snuggle times to share?
Then Cuddle Bear is made for you –
A hug-you-happy bear!

This panda needs a cuddle NOW! She's tripped and had a fright,

So Cuddle Bear comes scooting up...

A **hug** will put things right.

Poor Penguin's
missing all her friends,
Alone and far away,

But not too far
for Cuddle Bear

To bring a hug –
HOORAY!

The animals are scared of Lion,
He looks so big and wild.

He's **never,**
ever had a hug,
That's why he's
never smiled.

"We all need hugs!" says Cuddle Bear,
"However fierce we look."
Now Lion's happy as can be.
One hug was all it took!

Next Little Rabbit wants a hug,

A happy, bouncy one!

A squishy-squashy-squeezy hug
Is **super** cuddly fun!

It really doesn't matter,
If you're

BIG...

or short...

...or **tall,**

"A hug from me," says Cuddle Bear,
"Will stretch to fit you **all!**"

"The world needs hugs!" says Cuddle Bear,
"To make each day feel bright.
So stretch both arms and wrap them round
your friends to hug them tight!"

So now you know the secret!
Here's what you have to do...

Just hug the person that you love,
And they will hug you, too!

These Little Tiger books are made for you!

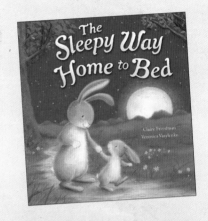

The Sleepy Way Home to Bed
Claire Freedman · Veronica Vasylenko

My Dad!
Steve Smallman · Sean Julian

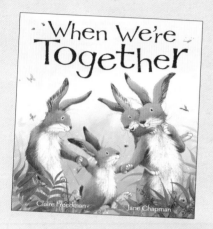

When We're Together
Claire Freedman · Jane Chapman

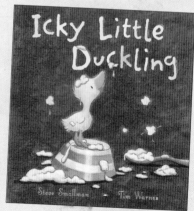

Icky Little Duckling
Steve Smallman · Tim Warnes

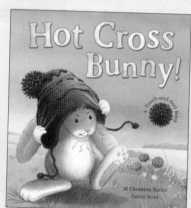

Hot Cross Bunny!
A Touch-and-Feel Book
M Christina Butler · Gavin Scott

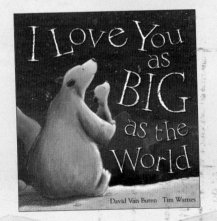

I Love You as BIG as the World
David Van Buren · Tim Warnes

For information regarding any of the above titles
or for our catalogue, please contact us:
Little Tiger Press, 1 The Coda Centre,
189 Munster Road, London SW6 6AW
Tel: 020 7385 6333 • Fax: 020 7385 7333
E-mail: info@littletiger.co.uk
www.littletigerpress.com